Lloyd Mifflin

Echoes of Greek Idyls

Lloyd Mifflin

Echoes of Greek Idyls

ISBN/EAN: 9783743383371

Manufactured in Europe, USA, Canada, Australia, Japa

Cover: Foto ©Andreas Hilbeck / pixelio.de

Manufactured and distributed by brebook publishing software
(www.brebook.com)

Lloyd Mifflin

Echoes of Greek Idyls

ECHOES

OF GREEK IDYLS

BY

LLOYD MIFFLIN

BOSTON AND NEW YORK
HOUGHTON, MIFFLIN AND COMPANY
The Riverside Press, Cambridge
1899

To

THE MEMORY

OF

THEOCRITUS

AN IDYL

Not in these valleys where we now recline,
　　But far beyond those purple peaks that glow,
　　Lies the fair land I love.　There winds are low
　　And soft.　He of the thyrsus and the vine
Comes with his leopards and his skins of wine.
　　Glimpses there are of Naiads to and fro
　　Flitting through groves ; and faint is heard and slow
　　The pipe of some brown Faun beneath the pine.
There upland streams, dissolving, reach the vales ;
　　And there are groves of ilex and of yew,
　　Unending valleys and Illyrian dales,
And gods reclining where the soft winds woo ;
　　And azure seas there are, and sunset sails,
　　And shepherds piping on the capes of blue.

CONTENTS

SELECTIONS FROM BION

BION

BION was a native of Smyrna, — one of the towns which claimed to be the birthplace of Homer.

I

WOE, woe for sweet Adonis, he is dead !
  The beauteous Adon, comely past compare !
  The lily youth with hyacinthine hair
  Low on the ground doth droop his princely head !
The hearts of all the Loves for him have bled.
  No more, O Cypris, filled with thy despair,
  In sleep thy purple raiment thou dost wear,
  But, sable-stoled, thy feet the shadows tread.
Arise, thou wretched one, oh, now arise !
  Make the air tremble with thy dolorous moan,
  And beat thy breasts and wail unto the skies :
" Gone is that golden voice of mellowest tone,
  Perished the love-light of his glowing eyes,
  And I am left all desolate and alone ! "

II

Upon the hills Adonis lieth low, —
    The wooded hills beneath the Idalian sky, —
    And all the wondrous whiteness of his thigh
    That looked as fair as newly-fallen snow,
Is by the boar's tusk gashed, and trickling slow
    The dark blood stains the ground with crimson dye;
    Heavy and dim now droops his fading eye,
    And marble-cold that ever beauteous brow.
His dying kiss has come to sudden pause, —
    That kiss that Cypris never would resign, —
    And from his face is paling out the rose;
For though his form her loving arms entwine,
    He cannot feel that with her breath she draws
    His very soul back ere it deathward goes.

III

Ah, cruel, cruel was his deadly wound,
  But in her heart doth Cytherea bear
  A deeper hurt than his who lieth there!
  The very dogs — each well-belovèd hound —
Bay o'er their master lying on the ground.
  And Aphrodite, now in her despair,
  Unsandaled, wretched, through the thorns that tear,
  Wanders and wails with tangled locks unbound.
Through the lone woodlands is her anguish borne;
  Lamenting him, she wildly raving goes,
  Calling his name, not once, but o'er and o'er;
While round his body, from his wound new-torn,
  The scarlet stream of life-blood spouting flows,
  Till all his blanchèd breast is dark with gore.

IV

Sᴏʀʀᴏᴡ her sacred beauty now doth slay;
   Her cup of grief is filled unto the brim;
   And Cypris' loveliness is growing dim
   Which, while Adonis lived, knew no decay.
Woe, woe for Cypris! all the mountains say;
   While all the oaks, from every ancient limb,
   Make solemn answer, *Woe, ah, woe for him!*
   And mourning fills the groves, and glooms the day.
The murmurous rivers purling in the vale
   Moan for lorn Aphrodite as they go,
   And weeping too are all the mountain wells;
The flowers in anguish red and redder grow,
   While Cytherea through the upland dells
   Shrills on the listening air her piteous wail.

V

FOR when she saw the wound of Adon bleed, —
   When she who loved him knew that he had died,
   With her the hardest heart had mourned and sighed,
   The end deploring of that bloody deed :
" Leave me not yet in this my bitter need ! "
   With arms aloft, she passionately cried ;
   " O my belovèd, stay — with me abide !
   Lip pressed to lip ! ah, hear me piteous plead !
Oh, wake, Adonis, do not from me go,
   Kiss me again, my sweet, the final kiss,
   Till from thy inmost heart deep into mine —
Into my very soul — thy love doth flow ;
   Kiss me again, O best beloved, divine,
   That I may drain the very depths of bliss ! "

VI

" THAT kiss which thou hast left me will I prize
    E'en as thyself, O thou most precious thing ! —
    Thou who must face dark Acheron's hateful king
    In realms Plutonian, far from mortal skies.
Wretched, forlorn, what means can I devise,
    Being a goddess, — ah, the cruel sting ! —
    To follow thee and to thy side to cling
    Where streams Lethean greet the wondering eyes ?

Take him, my lover, O Persephone,
    For thou, alas, art stronger far than I,
    And all of beauty drifts at last to thee ! —
Take thou my lord, who, fading, here doth lie ; —
    Lo, Sorrow sets her burning crown on me,
    And now all life seems but one lingering sigh ! "

VII

"Nay, I am widowed since that thou art gone,
  O thrice-desired, with thy comely grace, —
  Thou who didst love the dangers of the chase,
  Following thy hounds at earliest flush of dawn
While in the fern yet sleeps the dappled fawn.
  Thy death my beauty's girdle will efface ;
  In all the world none e'er can take thy place,
  Since thou art to the Stygian doors withdrawn."

.   .   .   .

Ah, for each drop the dying Adon bled,
  Upon the earth, like rain, her grief she showers,
  And all the groves are filled with sounds of rue ; —
Now that Adonis fair is cold and dead,
  The blood and tears bring forth two lovely flowers, —
  His blood, the rose ; her tears, the wind-flower blue.

VIII

" No more 'mid oaken woods, oh, now no more
　　May I lament for him and vainly weep ;
　　These forest leaves, new-gathered in a heap,
　　Not fitting are for one that I adore ;
Oh, let him have my couch, and, covered o'er,
　　Let him as erst the holy slumber keep,
　　Fair as a babe new-fallen into sleep, —
　　For e'en in death he is death's conqueror.
Strew wreathèd flowers dewy with the prime,
　　Upon the ground where he doth pale repose ;
　　Sprinkle his body with Assyrian nard
And fragrant spices of some Austral clime ; —
　　Nay, perish all sweet scents from my regard, —
　　He was my perfume, and my perfect rose ! "

IX

DRAPED in his purple raiment Adon lies,
  And near him Loves are weeping in the air;
  Sorrowing aloud, they clip their golden hair
  And drop the ringlets with suffusèd eyes;
And one the darts hath broke, 'mid tender sighs,
  Another, stooping, with the gentlest care
  Hath loosed the sandals of Adonis fair,
  While others, grieving, hover in the skies.
Many are sighing down the mournful wind,
  And round his pallid form are fluttering now;
  One laves the wound the cruel tusk did plow,
And still another, coming from behind,
  Draws near the dead, and piteously kind,
  Fans, with his little wings, Adonis' brow.

X

THE torches on the lintel of the door
    Hymen hath quenched and made to flicker down;
    And he hath torn to shreds the bridal crown,
    And Hymen's hymn is sung no more, no more!
Woe, woe for sweet Adonis, o'er and o'er
    The weepers sing, and mourn his bright renown;
    No gladness can their grief a moment drown; —
Woe, woe for Adon, whom they all deplore.
    .   .   .   .

Cease, Cytherea, from thy grieving sore,
    Weep thou for him again another year;
    For though the Muses call beseechingly,
He cannot come, in spite of prayer or tear; —
    No mortal voice he heeds on Pluto's shore
    Held in the shadows by Persephone.

THE HUSBANDMAN, THE FOWLER, AND LOVE

A FOWLER boy was hunting in the glade
   For merles and thrushes and the gentle dove,
   When on a box-tree bough the wingèd Love
   Perched, bird-like ; and the crafty hunter laid
His toils in vain, for, hopping, unafraid,
   The little restless Mischief did not move
   From out the shadow of the ilex grove.
   In hopeless quest the lad no longer stayed,
But, while his breast with anger sore was stirred,
   Sought out the teacher of his art, who said :
   "Give up the chase ; let the sly elf alone ;
Seek not to snare this evil-minded bird,
   For, though he shuns thee now, when thou art grown
   He 'll come uncalled, and settle on thy head ! ''

Once Cypris, leading Eros, said to me,
　"Kind Shepherd, take this boy I bring to you, —
　Teach him to sing as sweetly as you do."
　Straightway I showed him all my minstrelsy ; —
Played on the flutes, and took him on my knee ;
　How Hermes made the lyre, I told him, too,
　And how Apollo, god of music, drew
　From golden chords goldener melody.
Yea, all these things to Love I calmly taught,
　But he, not heeding, sang of man's desire —
　Of mortal's love, and of his mother's smiles.
Lo, I became the scholar, and I caught
　The soul of all his songs, and all their fire, —
　Forgot my teachings as I learned his wiles !

THE wild boy, Love, though full of all deceit,
   The Muses cherish and do never fear,
   But follow him their darling, doubly dear;
   From loveless-minded men, with hurrying feet
They flee away, nor teach them numbers sweet,
   Nor honeyed tones Pierian, golden-clear;
   But when one, love-smit, chaunts, they give hi
   And gladly run his joyous steps to greet.
A witness to this truth myself I bring,
   For if I venture upon other themes
   Sky-born or merely mortal, even then
My music falters in my breast; but when
   Of Lycidas and Love I gladly sing,
   Forth from mellifluous lips the carol streams!

Oh, if were doubled the brief mortal span
  Thro' the wise gods or by inconstant Fate, —
  Ah, could he spend one half in joy, elate,
  And one in labor under labor's ban,
Then he could toil, and after resting, man
  Might win reward ; but since is fixed his date,
  How heavy is the weary, weary weight
  Of burdens carried since his day began !
When wealth is won we covet wealth again ;
  Strangle our souls to lay base riches by ;
  Slave at laborious art, we know not why,
And go, alas — who guesses where or when ?
  How brief the hour allowed to mortal men !
  Do they forget they are condemned to die ?

O HESPER, golden light of eve serene,
   Lamp of the lovely daughter of the foam,
   Thou sacred jewel of the deep blue dome,
   Dimmer as much than Cynthia, silver queen, —
Who sinking slowly, yonder now is seen, —
   As thou art brighter than all stars that roam
   The skies ! oh, guide me to the shepherd's home
   The while I lead the revel o'er the green.
The moon wanes fast ; lend me thy beams divine,
   Illume the woods and dusky thickets nigh,
   Show me the way with thy refulgent light,
And bring me safely to my longed-for shrine ;
   No brigand, throttling travelers in the night,
   But a true lover, bent on love, am I.

MOTHER of Love, mild goddess, Cyprus-born,
   Daughter of Zeus, — though child of foam and wave, —
   Why 'gainst immortals and all men dost rave ?
   Nay, rant of them in bitterest, scathing scorn ?
Why wert thou so with passionate anger torn
   That thy most beauteous body erewhile gave
   Birth to that boy — the subtle, wicked knave —
   The heartless Love who makes the whole world mourn ?
Ah, why, sweet Cypris, didst thou give him wings
   And teach the wily god to shoot so far ?
   His cruel mind is so unlike his shape,
And calm of spirit he doth ever mar ;
   Child though he is, oh, we may ne'er escape
   The galling anguish of his bitter stings !

SELECTIONS FROM MOSCHUS

MOSCHUS

THE birthplace of Moschus is unknown.   He lived in the
age of Ptolemy Philadelphus, and was possibly contempo-
raneous with Theocritus.

CUPID, the rogue! — my darling runaway —
  Oh, who hath seen him where the cross-roads meet?
  His skin all blushing, and how honey-sweet
  His wily voice, I, Cypris, may not say!
More than a kiss from me shall be thy pay
  If thou return him; but, oh, be discreet,
  For on that saucy brow is writ deceit,
  And both his tongue and tiny hands betray!
If thou shouldst see him, bind, and hither bring
  The rosy scamp; but do not his desire, —
  Let not his lips to thine an instant cling!
And should he tempt with gift of arrows dire
  Or gilded bow, refuse each treacherous thing,
  For all his armature is dipped in fire!

I

To fair Europa, once upon a time,
    Sweet Cypris sent a mystic-laden dream :
    'T was in the third watch, when rare visions stream
    From out the dusky portals of the prime ;
When sleep, more sweet than honey or than rhyme,
    Lulls the lax spirit with some poppied theme
    That binds the eyelids in that soft demesne,
    When wingèd fancies float from other clime.
Then as the vision-bringing harbinger
    Stood by the threshold of the shadowy door
    Of virgin thoughts that trouble and perplex,
She saw two Continents at strife for her, —
    Asia the one, — one th' Hesperian shore :
    Both in the shape — but vaster — of her sex.

II

AND one of these had glorious, sorrowing eyes —
   She was the stranger, come from that far land;
   The other took Europa by the hand,
   Clung round her neck appealing in this wise:
" I nursed thee, child, and thee do idolize,"
   But still that other, 'neath her fillet-band,
   Reproving looked, and spake in high command:
   " By Zeus, fair maiden, thou shalt be my prize ! "
With beating heart in fear Europa sped
   Forth from her couch, so clear she viewed the dream —
   For, though awake, she saw the vision still ;
Then long upon her soft enticing bed
   Silent she sat, and, like a little stream
   Leaf-hid and timorous — some faint-hearted rill —

III

HER voice went trembling on in dazed surprise
    Sweet as the sacred brook Pierian :
    "Oh, who of all ye gods that mortals scan
    Hath sent these phantoms to my wondering eyes ?
Are these strange visions meant to terrorize ?
    Or do they herald some celestial plan
    Of happiness beyond the thought of man ?
    Who was the alien woman in such guise ?
For her a longing seizes on my heart ;
    How kind she looked, how graciously severe,
    As she my cheek unto her bosom drew !
It seemed as if I could not from her part :
    Ah, all ye blessèd gods, I pray you hear,
    Fulfill my dream, — oh, let it all come true !"

IV

THEN timid she arose and went to seek
  The maidens of her train — the lily girls
  Whose loosely-filleted and wandering curls
  Clustered around each glowing, rosy cheek;
Daughters that noble sires plain bespeak,
  With voices sweeter than the morning merles, —
  Fresh buds of rarest maidenhood, the pearls
  Of purple Tyre, — sea-crownèd queen antique.
In all Europa's sports they would engage,
  And their most beauteous bodies oft would they
  Bathe where the silver rivers meet the sea,
Or in the dance float on in bright array;
  Then on some flower-marauding pilgrimage
  Together pluck the lilies of the lea.

V

AND there she found her comrade-maidens dear
 Along the ocean on the rolling dunes,
 Where the spent sea leaves shallow blue lagoons
 That show the roots of rushes, amber-clear ;
Rare joy it was for them to wander here,
 For, though 't was morning, the full-orbèd moon's
 Pale face smiled down, and far they heard the tunes
 Sung by the surge across the sleeping mere.
And in her hand each maiden, o'er the leas,
 A basket bare, for roses they would cull ;
 But fair Europa's was of gold, inlaid,
Sculptured, embossed, by great Hephæstus made,
 Rich-wreathed with carven shapes of deities, —
 Once Telephassa's, and most wonderful !

VI

AND now the girls took ever fresh delight,
  As soon as on the meads their feet were set,
  In gathering flowers ; one the violet
  Divine and blue ; others the exquisite
Low-creeping thyme, and, in rich purple dight,
  The hyacinth ; or with a faint regret
  Dropt many a petal down all dewy-wet,
  Or culled the poet's flower — narcissus white.
But in the midst of this fair lily band,
  The Princess, with her ardent little hand,
  The sumptuous splendor of the scarlet rose
Plucked, lightly, with a touch imperial :
  Then queenly 'mid the graceful group she goes,
  And, like to Cypris, dwarfs her rivals all.

VII

THEN Zeus them seeing, changed himself at sight
   Unto a bull, Europa's love to gain :
   Not to such beast as in the burdened wain
   Beneath the yoke still sweats in sorry plight,
Feeds in the stalls, or from the dawn till night
   Drags on the curvèd plough in toilful pain, —
   Nay, but a bull of an immortal strain,
   Whose more than human eye doth love incite.
His lordly body brightest chestnut shone ;
   A silver star was set within his brow ;
   His looks with soft desire did importune ;
And from his foretop two branched horns were thrown,
   As when a flake of cloud divides the bow
   And leaves the two curves of the crescent moon.

VIII

HE came into the meadow in his pride
   Among the beauteous daughters gathered there;
   And they had yearnings deep to touch his hair
   And lay their white hands on his silken hide.
His heavenly fragrance round was wafted wide,
   Sweeter than perfume of the pastures fair;
   He closer drew, Europa to ensnare,
   And licked her cheek, and soft the virgin eyed.
Around his neck her arms she interwove,
   While from his mouth she wiped the foam that ran,
   And kissed his lips, by passionate love distraught;—
Against his spell the Princess vainly strove;—
   Then the bull lowed so sweetly, that you thought
   You heard the dulcet flute Mygdonian!

IX

HE bowed himself before her sandaled feet
   And bent his neck, and on the maiden gazed ;
   While his great loins enticed her and amazed ;
   Then gently did she her fair maids entreat :
"Come, dear my playmates, make my joy complete,
   Mount me upon the bull, and be not dazed,
   For ne'er a beast in fair Phœnicia grazed,
   So honest, mild, so gentle and discreet ! "
Then on his back, secure, she smiling sat
   And bade her rosy comrades follow too ;
   But from the ground great Zeus arose thereat —
Impelled by love's impetuosity —
   And, though she waved despairing hands in rue,
   On, like a dolphin, sped across the sea.

X

AND straight the tossed foam settled into blue,
  And waves were leveled in the ocean dells ;
  The dolphins tumbled in subsiding swells,
  And Nereids rode upon their sea-beasts too.
While he, the Shaker of the World, came through
  The briny paths whose ridgèd waves he quells,
  To guide his brother, where, with whorlèd shells
  The Triton trumpeters swept into view :
Round him they gathered in a joyous throng —
  With human torso and with dolphin tail —
  And in the wave their shining colors cast ;
Each lifted to his lips the sea-shell frail,
  And, as the bull-god and Europa passed,
  Blew from the raisèd conchs a bridal song !

XI

Meanwhile Europa on the bull divine
    Grew piteous pallid at her plight forlorn;
    While one hand clasp'd the great beast's glowing horn,
    The other in her mantle did entwine
Lest it should trail within the flying brine.
    The azure robe on her sweet shoulders worn,
    Puffed by the wind, sail-like, was backward borne,
    As sped they to the dim sea's far confine.
But when no longer landmarks could be seen, —
    Far from surf-beaten headlands of her home,
    Or lofty cliff well-loved, along the shore, —
When all was moving mounds and wastes of green
    With dark illimitable fields of foam,
    Her voice brake forth and this the wail it bore:

XII

" Oh, whither wilt thou bear me, wondrous bull ?
  How know'st the paths the ocean-monsters take ?
  What food is thine ? and what thy thirst doth slake ?
  Hast thou some spirit to guide thee like the gull,
And potency the rolling wave to lull ?
  The sea a path for flying ships doth make,
  But beasts for this their pastures ne'er forsake.
  Nay, thou art then some god most worshipful !
Lo, not the dolphin with his rainbow fin
  Fares on the land, nor kine upon the deep ;
  But fearless thou dost pass the sea and shores ;
Across the boundless-bosomed hyaline,
  And by the grottoes where the mermen sleep,
  With thy wild hoofs thou speedest as with oars !

XIII

" PERCHANCE then thou wilt rise above the air
   And speed on bird-like wings afar on high;
   Alas for me ! no marvel that I sigh,
   For my mischance is more than I can bear.
Far from my father's house I sadly fare ;
   It may be in the gray sea I shall die,
   For who could here a helpless maid descry ?
   Oh, lonely am I and I know not where !
Surely some deity will give me aid !
   Oh, thou the Shaker of the Earth, divine,
   Propitious come, and meet me on the wave —
Me, Telephassa's daughter, sore afraid —
   Surely I see thee coming me to save
   Who drop these tears in the unfeeling brine ! "

XIV

So moaned she, and the hornèd bull replied :
  "Take courage, maid, the dread deep dread not thou ;
  For Zeus am I, even I, — though veilèd now
  In semblance of a beast which thou dost ride ;
Still am I Zeus, and still am deified ;
  Ah, 't was the love of thy fair lily brow
  And bosom whiter than the Pelion snow
  That in this bovine made my godhead hide.
In Crete, that loometh there beyond the sea,
  With all her opulent dominion,
  There shall thy bridal bed be made, and then
Thou from the loins of Zeus — yea, even from me,
  Shalt bear great, golden-gifted, glorious sons,
  Sole sceptre-swaying monarchs over men !"

XV

So said the god, and voiced the words of fate :
    Soon o'er the wave the rim of Crete upreared ;
    And when the coast grew greener, and they neared
    The yellow sands, he donned his godhead straight,
And loosed the girdle of his lovely mate ;
    Then by their side the rosy Hours appeared
    To deck the bridal bed ; and, golden-sphered,
    The stars came out in more than regal state.

.   .   .   .

Mother she was of Minos called the Just —
    The king lawgiver by the Cretan seas,
    Who, later, judged the souls by Pluto's chair ;
Of Rhadamanthus of the Cyclades ;
    Sarpedon, who, self-banished, builded fair
    Miletus of far Caria, — long in dust.

I

WAIL, all ye woodlands and ye laureled glades,
   And low lament, thou azure Dorian deep !
   Ye silver rivers of Sicilia, weep, —
   For Bion, well-beloved, hath sought the shades !
Moan, all ye groves, along your dim arcades ;
   Ye lowly flowers, that in sad clusters creep
   Among the tangled wildwood, sink to sleep ;
   And as the touch of sorrow you invades,
O soft, ye roses, breathe yourselves away !
   Let the drooped petals of the hyacinth sigh,
   And murmur through the woods their *well-a-day ;*
Let blue anemones for grief turn red ;
   Yea, all green things that grow, despair and die, —
   For he, the dulcet Singer, now is dead !

II

Oh, all ye liquid-throated nightingales
    Singing among the dusk leaves of the trees,
    Pour forth your lamentable elegies
    Along the twilight of Sicilian dales !
Reiterate, ye birds, your lovelorn tales !
    Murmur your sorrows to the evening breeze
    Where Arethusa, from across the seas,
    Listens beside the fountain in your vales !
For him, who sang like you his deathless songs,
    O swans Strymonian, chaunt some dolorous dirge
    Immortal and melodious as his own !
Not to the Thracian Nymphs he now belongs,
    For he hath passed beyond the Stygian verge, —
    This Dorian Orpheus of mellifluous tone !

III

No more at eve unto his kine he sings, —
 The well-belovèd herdsman passed away ;
 No more beneath the oaks, at dawn of day,
 One hears afar his dulcet carolings ;
By Pluto's side he chaunts of other things, —
 Oblivion, and the fate of mortal clay ;
 Ah, nevermore his gladsome roundelay
 Shall sound in upland pastures by the springs !
The heifers wander by the bulls forlorn
 With many an anxious and grief-laden low,
 Nor will they touch the wealth of clover-deeps ;
The mountains, too, are voiceless, eve and morn ;
 The flocks are silent on the silent steeps,
 Listening for him who fluted long ago !

IV

PÆAN himself lamented thy sad doom,
   O Bion, master of sweet minstrelsy!
   And e'en the uncouth satyrs mourned for thee;
   The garden gods, amid the dittany bloom,
Wore sable stoles to semble forth their gloom;
   The fountain fays beneath the ilex-tree
   Rivers of tears are weeping ceaselessly,
   And even Echo grief doth now consume.
In anguish for thy fall, the orchard trees
   Let drop their fruit throughout the silent vale,
   And sorrow blights the beauty of the rose;
Since thou art gone dark waves the galingale,
   No milk hath flowed from udders of the ewes,
   Nor is there honey in the comb of bees.

V

Oh, not the swallows on the ridges high,
   Nor plaintive note of piteous Philomels,
   Nor dolphins rolling in the ocean swells
   About the sea-banks, nor, in summer sky,
The halcyon shrilling forth her mournful cry,
   Nor that strange bird of Memnon in the dells
   Of dawn, e'er sang such touching, sad farewells
   As were poured forth, when, Bion, thou didst die!
O all ye swallows he once gave delight, —
   Taught you to twitter and almost to talk —
   There as ye sit together on the bough,
Mourn low for him ; ah, all ye warblers bright,
   And nightingales in every bosky walk,
   Bemoan yourselves he is not with you now!

VI

Who, Bion, who would dare to be so bold
    As press his lips to thy mute instrument?
    Since thou art gone, who so irreverent
    To try his sleight on that rare pipe of gold?
For still from thy dead mouth the tune is rolled
    Along the pastoral valleys, redolent
    Of thee, and with thy beauteous spirit blent, —
    For there thy name is fragrant as of old.
And shall we let Pan try thy hushed pipe now
    Since far thou wanderest in immortal meads?
    Nay, even he, remembering, would refuse,
Lest he should touch the stops less sweet than thou!
    Oh, never will the world thy warblings lose,
    For Echo croons them standing 'mid her reeds.

VII

E'EN Galatea loved thy song divine, —
    The lily, who in sweet Sicilian lands
    Clasped Acis, crushed to death at Cyclop's hands; —
    Not on the sea-banks now doth she recline;
She hath forsaken the cerulean brine,
    And sitting lonely on the lonely sands,
    Seeing unherded all thy lowing bands,
    She thinks on thee and keeps thy wandering kine.
Now Cypris more thy memory enjoys
    Than that last kiss by Adon's wounded side;
    Sadly the loves are mourning round thy tomb;
Ah, all desired gifts with thee have died, —
   The blissful mouths of maidens in their bloom,
    And lovely kisses from the lips of boys!

VIII

MELES, most musical of rivers, flow,
    In this thy second sorrow, to the sea ;
    Homer — that sweet mouth of Calliope —
    Thou once didst lose ; and now this newer woe,
The Herdsman's death, — thou hast to undergo ;
    Wail, River, wail for him unceasingly,
    For nevermore from reedy pipe shall he
    Flute his soft Dorian adagio !
Ah, not of wars he sang, and not of tears,
    But of the shepherds and of Pan would chaunt
    Among the pastures sweeter than a bird ! —
Would gather rushes in some marshy haunt,
    And make the pipes that still his song endears,
    Or, rising, milk the heifers of the herd.

IX

PINDAR and Hesiod are regretted less
　Than thou, O Bion, in Bœotian woods;
　And not in Lesbos and her solitudes,
　Alcæus and thy lovelorn poetess
Cause, by their death, such utter hopelessness.
　Not for Archilochus the lone Nymph broods
　Deeper in Paros by th' Ægean floods;
　Nor light is Mytilene's new distress.
　.　.　.　.　.　.　.　.　.

Famed was Theocritus of Syracuse,
　But unto Bion doth my dirge belong,
　Who am no alien to the pastoral lute;
To me, when Bion died, he left his Muse —
　To me, a singer of Ausonian song —
　The deathless heritage of the Doric flute.

X

Ah me, when all the garden mallows fade
    And drop their petals with a seeming sigh;
    When beds of parsley green begin to dry,
    And tendrils of the anise low are laid
Withering upon the walks, we ne'er upbraid, —
    For if, when Winter comes, they seem to die,
    We smile within our hearts, for by and by
    Spring will remake them as the Spring has made.
But oh, we men, the mighty, and the wise,
    Inheritors of splendors gone before, —
    We men, when once into the earth we go,
We meet the irremediable woe;
    In darksome graves we close unseeing eyes
    In dreamless sleep, that waketh nevermore!

XI

As evil men will lay a deadly bait
  And kill the sweetest of the singing birds,
  So, Bion, envious of thy honeyed words,
  They poisoned thee because of rancorous hate.
Ah, who so basely could thy death predate ?
  Thee who could harm that knew thy song of herds,
  Of kid and kine, of milkings and of curds ? —
  No music lived within the vile ingrate !
But for this deed which still my soul o'erwhelms —
  Thy death by lowest among craven men —
  They shall be judged by justice, whom they scorn,
And swift condemned in Rhadamanthus' realms :
  But I shall never hear thy voice again
  Fluting upon the hills, at eve or morn !

XII

IF I, by my deep passion rendered bold,
  Had sought the gloom of that Plutonian shore,
  Like him, the famèd lion conqueror,
  Or that rare lyrist of the harp of gold,
Or wise Ulysses of the days of old, —
  I might, within that dark and Stygian door,
  Have heard if there thou still didst sweetly pour
  Thy rich Sicilian pastorals manifold.

There Dis shall drop his keys and dream of vales
  He trod in Enna once, on hearing thee ;
  And ah, what grief will touch Persephone
When that thou pipest of her long-lost dales ! . .
  But as to earth came back Eurydice,
  Mayst thou return among our nightingales !

"As a bird mourning for her nestlings dead,
   Killed in the boscage by some serpent vile,
   Flutters around her little fledglings, while
   Her piteous note fills all the grove o'erhead, —
But cannot bring the life back that is sped,
   Yea, fears herself the reptile's fang and guile,
   And wails the loss she ne'er can reconcile,
   For all the comfort of her heart is fled, —
So hath this soul been harrowed — even mine;
   The children so beloved — that beauteous brood —
   By my dear lord were killed before these eyes,
And all the floor swam crimson with their blood.
   Ah, woe is me, who childless here repine;
   Now naught is left but never-ending sighs!"

BY THE GRAY SEA

WHEN all unruffled sleeps the silent sea,
　　Outward I look, and love the land no more;
　　Fain would my feet forever leave the shore
　　To drift upon that calm serenity.
But when wild ocean thunders angrily,
　　And torn waves break into white foam, and roar,
　　Then I, ill pleased, seeking the greenwood floor,
　　Love the wind's harping through each swaying tree.
Ah, he whose life is passed upon the wave,
　　Whose wandering bark is but a house of death,
　　Toils through wild dangers to a watery grave:
Me, rather, let the forest lull to dreams,
　　Low lying on some bank, the boughs beneath,
　　In calm repose beside the woodland streams.

By Pisa, forth Alphèus ardent flows
   Through Arcady to the Ionian brine,
   Past many a shepherd piping 'neath the pine ;
   Deep through the emerald wave he swiftly goes
Bearing his bridal gifts of laurel and rose
   And sacred soil and sprays of eglantine :
   Headlong he rushes to that fountain shrine —
   Fair Arethusa — with his lover's woes !
His currents, under Ocean, miles and miles
   Unmingling wind, until they disembogue
   In far Ortygia, fresh and sparkling free.
Ah, thus hath Love, the mischief-making rogue,
   The teacher of all knavish, artful wiles,
   Taught even a river to run beneath the sea !

SELECTIONS FROM BACCHYLIDES

BACCHYLIDES

BACCHYLIDES, a native of Ceos, and nephew of Simonides, was a rival of Pindar, and was considered one of the masters of lyric poetry. He lived about 500 B. C. The recent discovery of the Egyptian papyri containing some of his Odes gives an added interest to his name at this time. The exquisite fragment on Peace was, until this discovery, the longest production of his known to exist.

I

TO HIERO, OF SYRACUSE, WINNER OF THE RACE

THOU canst be judge, if any mortal may —
   High-destined King of golden Syracuse —
   Of honeyed music flowing from the Muse ;
   And now, at rest awhile from sceptred sway,
Turn hither, listen to these strains, and say
   If the fair-cinctured Graces do infuse
   Aught of their charm unto these words I choose,
   Who come from Zea's isle to tune this lay.
And if Bacchylides — such votary I
   Of golden-filleted Urania — dare
   In verse that race unparalleled to sing,
Won at Olympia by thyself, O king,
   Be thou the judge, as thou art just and fair,
   And hear me hymn thy royal praises high !

II

THE EAGLE

ALOFT, and cleaving the ethereal air
   With tawny wings, far in the dazzling skies,
   The Eagle of the Thunderer grandly flies
   Where other glorious soarers fear to dare;
Not the cloud-piercing peaks, snow-crowned, that glare,
   Nor the torn ocean that man terrifies
   Balk his free plume nor daze his dauntless eyes, —
   Imperious and imperial past compare!
Still onward, upward through the regions dread,
   Companioned by the wind above the seas,
   Mounting in splendor sweeps the king of birds:
I, too, have empyrean paths to tread,
   To chaunt your praises in, and wingèd words,
   O sons illustrious of Dinomenes!

III

PHERENICUS — A HIPPOPÆAN

CALL that man blest to whom the skies concede
  A share of triumph from the multitude ;
  No mortal path is always flower-bestrewed, —
  But happy he whom pomp and station lead :
Thy horse, O Hiero, the storm-footed steed,
  The fiery Pherenicus, chestnut-hued,
  Was, near Alphèus' river, early viewed
  Victorious, and on haunted, Delphian mead.
Matchless he was for conquest, — failure-proof, —
  For by the holy Earth I swear it true,
  That, as he furious swept anear the goal,
No dust could touch him of a rival hoof ;
  Swift as the wild-blown north-wind on he flew
  Amid the shouts the nations loud uproll !

I

MEDEA TO ÆGEUS

" O ÆGEUS, of the soft Ionians, lord,
    And king of Athens, why these notes of war?
    Does the harsh trumpet of some conqueror —
    Crossing the frontier vast and unexplored,
To devastate the land with fire and sword —
    Sound on the air? — Some rash conspirator
    Who leaves the shepherds lying in their gore
    And adds their flocks, new-stolen, to his hoard?
For if not this, O King, then what alarms
    Thy soul?   Tell me, of Circe's line, thy friend;
    For thou who art the glorious warrior-son
Of great Pandion, — thou hast men and arms,
    And power supreme o'er thy dominion,
    With glittering hosts thy borders to defend."

II

ÆGEUS TO MEDEA

" A HERALD, hurrying through the day and night,
  From the extremest border brings the news
  Of wondrous deeds — of him of mighty thews,
  Who kills tree-bending Sinis in his might,
Slays the man-slaying Crommyon boar at sight,
  Spears Sciron by the sea, and then pursues
  And lets death give brute Cercyon his dues, —
  Which ends the wrestling giant's cruel sleight;
Aye, strong Procrustes that in iron bed
  Stretches the travelers that come anear
  Until the hapless ones for mercy sue,
He conquers, — these, and more besides are dead:
  What else may not this alien wonder do?
  By Zeus! then think you we have naught to fear?"

III

MEDEA TO ÆGEUS

"But did the Herald give the stranger's name?
  Whence sprung? and if he brought an armèd force?
  Comes he empanoplied? with myriad horse?
  With clarion pealing, and with loud acclaim?
Or singly, yet with daring strength to tame
  These potent ones he vanquished in his course?
  Intrepid must he be, — of vast resource,
  Who all alone such mighty foes o'ercame!
Or is he some bright creature of the sky
  With heaven's mission in the world to fill, —
  Dispenser of the vengeance of the gods?
It must be, else, in battling, his great skill
  Should at the last meet with some fearful odds
  Fatal to him; this, time will verify."

IV

ÆGEUS TO MEDEA

" THESE words the Herald brought : ' The warrior stands
   With but two men beside him ; and there gleams
   A sword from shining shoulders ; glittering beams
   Play round twin polished javelins in his hands ;
A Spartan helmet clasps his hair in bands ;
   He wears a purple tunic as beseems
   His rank ; a mantle of Thessalia streams
   Across that breast high courage still commands.
Oh, youth sits thronèd in each lineament !
   His eyes red flames flash like to Ætna's cone ;
   And where the battle's clangor calls afar
He plays the joyous game of crimson war ;
   And even now his vengeful feet are bent
   For splendor-loving Athens and its throne.' "

ILLUSTRIOUS he who binds his auburn hair
    With wreaths triennial.   Fortune hath such boon
    Granted Automedes, and newly strewn
    His path with victory — the athlete fair,
Preëminent, as in the azure air
    Of some cerulean-vaulted night of June
    In her full glory is the orbèd moon.
    The amazèd crowd pressed round at him to stare, —
The wondrous discus-hurler, true and bold,
    Unmatchable in all the wrestling bouts, —
    For with his brawn a nameless grace was blent ;
And when the javelin through the sky he sent,
    The assembled hosts of Hellas raised such shouts
    As might have waked Enceladus of old !

I

As when on darkening seas the north-wind blows
  Furious and wild, and the white-crested waves
  Threaten the mariners with watery graves
  Who on the midnight deck unconscious doze,
Then with the opening of the Auroran rose
  The south-wind bellies all the sails, and paves
  The sea-paths blue around the mermaid caves
  And full of hope to port the sailor goes :
So the sad Trojans, when they heard that grim
  Achilles lingered yet within his tent
  Sporting with sweet Briseis, yellow-haired, —
Rejoiced, and gladness through their legions went ;
  No longer felt they dreadful fear of him,
  War's cloud was lined with light, and none despaired.

II

THEN from the walls they rushed unto the shore,
  And by the ship's stern fought anear the flood,
  Where furious Hector with his victims' blood
  Stained the soil dark, while all the waters bore
The tint of carnage, and both sail and oar
  Were crimson splashed. . . Ah, fools, to think they c
  Despoil those blue-prowed ships with havoc rude,
  And on the morrow shouts victorious pour
Along the god-built streets of Ilion !
  But they were counting without fate's decree,
  And Nemesis and her avenging powers, —
For they were doomed, before that time, to see
  With Trojan blood Scamander's waters run,
  Reddened by overthrowers of their towers.

To Phere's son these words Apollo told :
    " One of two omens may thy lot assuage, —
    That thou shalt die to-morrow, or thy age
    Be lengthened many a year till thou be old."
Live just and joyous ; greet the cheerer, gold.
    No stain the sun in all his pilgrimage
    Finds in the sky ; no one, though wisest sage,
    Through time to youth can e'er be backward rolled.
But virtue hath a radiance all her own,
    Which dims not as ephemeral deeds of man,
    Nor pales as doth the fleeting star of fame ;
'T is nurtured at the holy Muse's flame
    And shines forever, as it still hath shone,
    White as the deathless gods Olympian !

THEN Menelaus to persuade them, spake:
 " Warriors of Troy, 't is not high-ruling Zeus
 That is the cause of all this world's abuse,
 For men are free the paths of right to take.
Justice, chaste Order, and the Law, these make
 Man blest. Ah, happy they whose children choose
 These dwellers in their streets! They only lose
 Who basely gain, — who faith and honor break.
And they who through contempt of equal rights
 Court Arrogance and her pernicious train, —
 Bestowing gifts they never truly owned, —
Though girt by flaming suns, yet walk in night's
 Abysmal darkness; — and it was her reign
 That shook earth's kingdoms, and her kings de-
  throned!"

O PEACE, what blessings come in thy sweet name !
   Plenty from earth, and poesy from the skies ;
   For the immortals, thou dost bring the thighs
   Of oxen and the long-wooled sheep that flame
On fiery altars ; the athletic game,
   The flute, the dance, and youth's festivities :
   In hand-holds of the shield, the spider lies
   And weaves her web ; spear-points that overcame
The warrior in the battles' red retreats,
   And two-edged swords, all rust, and rest from war.
   No brazen clarion of the conqueror
Comes now caressing slumber to impair,
   But joyous revelry doth fill the streets,
   And notes of love-lays linger in the air.

NOTES

NOTES

THE prefatory sonnet in this book, entitled *An Idyl*, is here reprinted from the volume of Sonnets, *At The Gates of Song*.

PAGE 5.   The beautiful myth of Adonis originated in Asia, and perhaps typifies the decay of nature in autumn and its renewal in the spring ; — the wild boar being a symbol of the cold and ruthless winter.

PAGE 25.   It has been the aim to retain the Greek proper names throughout these versions; but in this instance the word Cupid has been used, — it being endeared to all hearts.

PAGE 26.   The reader need scarcely be reminded that in this beautiful Idyl Europa personifies the broad-spreading light of morning, born of the dawn, and traveling to her home in the western sky.

PAGE 36.

> Or sweet Europa's mantle blew unclasped,
> From off her shoulder backward borne :
> From one hand drooped a crocus : one hand grasped
> The mild bull's golden horn. — *Tennyson.*

PAGE 40.   The Idyl of Moschus ends at the seventh line of this Sonnet.

PAGE 49.   Where the break occurs in this sonnet after the octave, seven stanzas are missing in the Idyl.

Line 13.   So Spenser in *The Ruines of Rome :* —

> " By which th' Ausonian light may be restored."

Page 50. Wordsworth, in one of his sonnets, seems to have imitated Moschus : —

> " While we the brave, the mighty and the wise,
>   We men, who in our morn of youth defied
>   The elements, must vanish ; — be it so ! "

PAGE 54. This sonnet, written in 1897, is here reproduced from *The Slopes of Helicon*, it being one of the Moschus series. It will be seen from the following sonnet that the author has used part of Shelley's second line : —

TRANSLATION FROM MOSCHUS

IDYL V

BY PERCY BYSSHE SHELLEY

WHEN winds that move not its calm surface sweep
  The azure sea, I love the land no more.
  The smiles of the serene and tranquil deep
  Tempt my unquiet mind. — But when the war
Of ocean's grey abyss resounds and foam
  Gathers upon the sea, and vast waves burst,
  I turn from the drear aspect to the home
  Of earth and its deep woods, where interspersed,
When winds blow loud pines make sweet melody.
  Whose house is some lone bark, whose toil the sea,
  Whose prey the wandering fish, an evil lot
Has chosen. — But I my languid limbs will fling
  Beneath the plane, where the brook's murmuring
  Moves the calm spirit but disturbs it not.

PAGE 73. Lines 7–8. More than two centuries after Bacchylides, Theocritus, in the sixteenth Idyl, invoking peace for his beloved Sicily, uses the same image : —

" May spiders weave their gauzy webs over all martial weapons, and may none, henceforth, so much as name the shout of onset ! "